Jigs and Reels

Jigs and Reels

Short Prose by **Michael Stephens**

Hanging Loose Press
Brooklyn, New York

Published by Hanging Loose Press
231 Wyckoff Street
Brooklyn, New York 11217

Hanging Loose Press thanks the Literature Programs of the
National Endowment for the Arts and the New York State
Council on the Arts for grants in support of the publication of
this book.

Acknowledgments: Some of these pieces first appeared in the
following magazines, for which the writer wishes to thank the
editors: *Pequod, Paris Review, Paragraph, Fiction Magazine,
Hanging Loose,* and *Fiction International.*

First Printing
Printed in the United States of America

Cover art: *Elephant Drum* by Archie Rand, from The Perform-
ance Series. Collection of Richard Dunn.

Library of Congress Cataloging-in-Publication Data

Stephens, Michael Gregory.
    Jigs and reels / Michael Stephens.
        p.   cm.
    ISBN 0-914610-86-4 : — ISBN 0-914610-85-6 (pbk.) :
    I. Title.
    PS3569.T3855J5   1991
    811'.54—dc20   91-44137
                                                                       CIP

Produced at The Print Center., Inc., 225 Varick St.,
New York, NY 10014, a non-profit facility for literary
and arts-related publications. (212) 206-8465

TABLE OF CONTENTS

FOR RUSSELL BANKS,
my Jersey rabbi

FOOTSTEPS

I waited until after four, listening for your footsteps I can't tell, there was some wine I drank away, leaving the other cup for you, I had something for you, a bundle a drawing, of what I thought it was you were, my ashtrays filled, I'm going home, and I want you to know that I waited and waited, leaving, I left, and left this note...

SHEETS

The laundry flaps in the wind like wings. And her skirts ride up like sheets, her legs bared and holding the grass. Her face rides up into the sky as though she were the wind.

THE IRIS

The child picked up the iris, fallen in the grass, purple and yellow, part caterpillar, part tiger, its petals already peeled back with decay, and within days, dark on the mantelpiece, it withered—withered and stunk—so beautiful and yet it smelled like a midden of beauty, and when she picked it up again, her mother grabbed it, flushing it away...

SAFEHOUSE

The loner out of Rangoon—double agent, agent provocateur, secret agent—tracks his leads from Singapore to the Khyber Pass, smoking endless cigarettes as he waits for information. He knows the world from Greenwich east to the date line, marking time on his Rolex watch, recording images on his Rolleiflex camera, he travels under diplomatic cover, passing secrets like a dinner guest passes butter or wine, with caution and politesse, urbanity, the microdots scatter from the pepper shaker, the information is culled, evidence is raked, information digested, then shredded. He carries a gun with a silencer, a cyanide pill, a long knife as blue as a razor. Spy to spy, he is lured to this oriental woman in a trench coat and big green hat, their meetings never licit, never discussed outside the safehouse, they meet lover to lover, with lives which do not exist beyond these walls, for they never talk about the world outside the safehouse, a sublime cover, not a Grand Hotel which would be a mark of indiscretion, it is a tiny unbugged apartment here in Bangkok, down the street from *Le Bebe Club*. He undresses and she steps naked from her trench coat—secrets exchanged, whispers, fumblings for cigarettes, the steady ripple of whiskey over ice—within the hour they depart for other ports, other cities, new assignments, with promises to meet again shortly.

THE BALL PEEN HAMMER

Dear Alice: Because of love, I hammered away at you, and because I enjoy the motion, the emotion, and the commotion it makes with the neighbors. Once I thought a rubber mallet slammed against my own head might induce sleep or new forms of conscience, or make me conscious of the day. Ha! I am finished with bland nights, these warmed-over blandishments, and prefer the steel of hammer to the crush of bone in the skull. I peen my own head, then peen your skull, laughing all the while, as though I were funnier than Desi and Lucy, Bud and Lou, Imogene and Sid, or even Ed and Trixie. We are our own kind of variety show, and relatives come to watch, videotaping the proceedings. Once I had found the ball peen hammer, I peened the walls of our house, the windows, the floorboards, and I shouted to passersby: This is for love, and I do this because I am in love, I am a lover. Yours, Ralph. P.S. Norton and I are going bowling tonight.

KNIVES

Many spoons in the sink, and that means it was a dull night, too much coffee and ice cream, not enough foreplay. If there are many forks, it was probably a good night. But most importantly if there were many knives used, it was a great night, even if misunderstandings arose, people were stabbed, blood flowed. Spoons suggest measuring. After most suicides, detectives discover many spoons in the sink. There may be one knife that killed a person, but it is merely a symbol of too many spoons and forks: a wish for knives at table. Eliot was wise about spoons measuring life; even Edgar Lee Masters saw their monotony well enough. All those sentimental songs about "spooning." Even what spoon rhymes with is worthless; moon, June, croon. Spoon never rhymes with wife the way knife does. Forks are frequently connected with a type of sex, but what this type is—no one knows. And even the fork has a kind of character which can't be denied, and yet it is not the mark of an outstanding evening. The happy household is spoonless; but don't be fooled by chopsticks. Houses need knives. Families depend on knives to survive. A man may eat peas off a knife; he may drink blood from it. A sink filled with knives is a house that has had an eventful dinner.

COUNTRY WESTERN

A motorcyle going seventy-five miles per hour—45 mph over the speed limit, that is—burns through the amber warning lights on the one main street of the town. Black, his gloves, black his helmet, his boots, his beard, his jacket, his bike. It is five o'clock in the afternoon, the sun still high up in the sky. The stink of rubber from his tires fills the town with a bouquet. Inside the bar, those men there watch the biker pass. One says: "Now that one's a mother's son," and all nod, all agree. "Give this man another beer," a third shouts, gesturing to the person next to him. "Set up the rest of the bar on me," another shouts. The mill was shut two years ago, and the town's water supply is tainted. Old veterans and young veterans sit together, their differences about World War II, Korea, and Vietnam at an end. Now they see eye to eye, all of them out of work and no longer receiving benefit checks. The television news tells of faraway places like Central America, the build-up of troops at the borders. One of the youngest vets says: "I thought I would never say this, but ever since I've been out of work, I miss old Nam." Another round is drunk and another is bought, whoever has the money today pays for the others, who will pay for him on that day when he is without funds. This time the bartender treats them all. They hold their longneck beer bottles and swivel around in their seats, they all look out the window, as though the lone black biker might come zooming back into town. But the driver and his motorcycle are long gone...

STARLINGS

They were like the starlings on the bare winter lawns near the park, scavenging for crumbs and ashes, twittering, turning star-like in the mid-afternoon, and by evening they flew away, leaving only the local dogs and the sparrows, the pigeons and no more. I turned such a corner, thinking of these things, every day turning that corner, approximately at the same time of day, before the sun goes down, passing along minding myself, not annoying anyone, stepping between the panhandlers and the drifters, the single-room-occupancy people and the man in his wheelchair, that crying, dirty-faced young woman always begging for handouts for her dog and when she got them, hitting the dog and telling it to shut up, between the streetwalker and the hawker, between old Latin mothers and their children, old men out of Lublin and young men fresh out of college, and when I turned that corner, thinking that a man who drinks beer turns into beer, or one who drinks whiskey, sitting for long periods on a barstool, turns into whiskey and then the barstool, I turned into the corner, becoming this neighborhood. (It took about ten years for this to happen.) The other day I watched others turn the corner in the opposite direction, crossing the street, and heading toward the promenade, single file, two abreast, or none at all, chatting about their relatives in Jersey or those in eastern Europe four decades ago, themselves barely escaping by steamer to this world, one of them saying, If you think you're lucky, then you're lucky, and you think this life a burden, it is, and his friend answering, If you think, if you think, Max, all you do is think and all I do is think, so what else is new? That moon, Max answered, that's new, and when is the last time you saw it this early up in the sky, right here in the afternoon, that's new, too, and so is this hat with the red feather in it, and so is this raincoat, which I got for practically nothing when that nice old store on the corner went out of business after fifty years, I remember buying my first jacket there when I was a young man, right off the boat and my uncle gave me the money to buy it, he said, Max, you need to look good if you want to find work and I know you'll make it up to me someday, which I did, a thousand times over, but never regretting it, because my Uncle Ben saved my life, and he saved my mother and father, my sister Esther, without him, where would I be, I tell myself, and later I met my wife Celeste on that corner, what red hair, and she turned into an old woman, and she turned again, turning and listening to me say this, turning and turning to dust...

GRANDMOTHERS

1.

From my first memory of her, she was gray-haired and always wore black, she had a pillbox hat, which she stuffed on the top of her head, and in winter she wore a black long wool coat which reached almost to her swollen ankles, and always she wore the black shoes (sensible ones) with a small heel. She was four foot eight and had the largest bosom of any woman I have ever seen, then or now, and a swelling to her joints everywhere. Her hands were like a porcelain doll's. She did not curse, she prayed. She prayed for all of us, living and dead, and she scolded the children when they misbehaved. Her smell was Seven-Eleven, her eyes dark, her skin white, her lips handsome and her nose hawkish. Her hair was tied into a bun, which she let down to comb at the beginning and end of each day, and when it unraveled, her hair reached to the floor. She told me once that it had never been cut in her life, and after combing it out and putting it back into a bun, we went out to the seven o'clock mass up the block, the one Monsignor Lowe said, first thing every morning. After church, Grandma told me that I had a calling, a calling, she said, and I should become a Maryknoll missionary or at least a Franciscan like her own youngest son, but I interrupted her by saying that it was a school day and I had to get home for breakfast or I would be late. In the late afternoon, she and my mother tooted on the red wine, and grandma said, "We live so long in my family because we have a glass of wine every day and take an aspirin." When she died, she was ninety, broken hip, Flatbush, and at her funeral, I saw her bone white face, still wrinkleless—"the Noxzema," she once told me—and my wife asked how an old woman like her had no wrinkles?

2.

Technically, she wasn't even my grandmother because she was my father's stepmother, but we got along like bloods whenever I stayed at her apartment in East New York on Macdougal

10

Street. The old man had several stories about his real mother. He used to say that she died when their apartment on the Upper West Side of Manhattan burned to the ground on Christmas Eve. Later he said she died in her thirties from stomach cancer, and out in Brooklyn. Nothing was ever said about his father, though, and he didn't have too many words for this woman I called grandmother, either. Imagine mackerel stink and poteen, potatoes and the salmon-happy rivers as her girlhood. But as a grown woman, she never got beyond this apartment in Brooklyn. She called me Mickey, and hobbled about the flat on her one good leg, the other amputated from gangrene. This one-legged old gal drank her beer by the quart, and after a few in the morning, her head out the window to the produce man in his horse-drawn cart, she shouted, "Ye gobshite foockin bastard banana boat refugee, if I had two legs I'd bash your face good, Guido, ye snipe, ye shite, ye evil foocker, I'll collar ye yet, and break your bones, I'll mash you into peet, and rip off your eyeballs to boot and cook 'em like taters," and then taking a breath, she said, "now give me me produce before I git angry," and the banana man was so intimidated by her that he gave her what she asked for and more, and all of it at discount, maybe even half the price, and he undercharged her every day of her life in Brooklyn for the fear inside of him about the old one-legged gal with her tits like watermelons leaning out the first story window. Then she died. Like that. And the stupid ones had malt and hops, beer and whiskey at her wake, wailing and laughing and singing in that funeral parlor on Broadway, right across from Our Lady of Lourdes, where Mother Teresa's girls live today...

NIRVANA NERVOSA

It is not so much that life is *nothing*, life *is* nothing, but that
besides that, it is also everything, everything besides, not so
much hell, for it is not eternal, it ends, thank god, one day the
wires fizzle, the head lops over into the lap, and the peas spill
from the mouth, rolling over the table like billiard balls, the eyes
go gaga, and comes that famous death rattle, really more a gur-
gle, the last spit, a spurt of saliva, enzymes, juices, or then there
is going to sleep, dying in a dream, never waking, that is most
frightening, the thought of dying, not really dying, but those
moments before when the end is assured, is imminent, upon us
and then the twenty gun salute, the hangman enters or perhaps
it is a friend or lover, a child looking for ice cream, there is dying
in restaurants, and, most ignoble of all, being burst through the
windshield of a speeding car which happens to be careening
over an embankment with a ten-wheel drive truck heading
down right between the eyes, no, life is not hell, because it is
finite, but it would be hell were it infinite, so that now let's only
call it purgatory, temporary pain, but thoroughgoing, intense,
with letup, letdown, terrifying, like those moments late at night
when sleep has flown to the wind, the eyes are electric and
every miscalculated heartbeat, whisper, every creak of the bed
or floorboard is the end, thank god, but then comes a sort of
dream, a suspended state in which life and death are held in
abeyance, at odds, invariably congested by darkness insinuat-
ing itself into the body of the sleeper who is dreamlessly tense
or the non-sleeper who is dreaming he is dead, he died, the
woman said, he was laying next to me and the next thing I
knew, his heart stopped, we held a mirror under his nose and
there was no mist, his hands grew cold, gray, rock-like, and I
screamed, I let out this piercing scream, but we were vacation-
ing in the woods, there wasn't a person around for miles and
outside the cabin I saw animal tracks leading to a clearing, an
apple orchard, or maybe just a meadow somewhere, and those
doe-like eyes multiplying in the night, a million animal eyes
upon me as that man lay next to me, frozen, petrified, gone for
good, so I lay back on my cool pillow, I lit a cigarette and I

thought about what I would do next, what would I do, I said, what can I do now, I haven't worked in years, I've grown soft, foggy, indifferent, and we never worried about saving money or anything, I just smoked a cigarette and thought about blowing out my brains with his rifle or tearing out my eyes with the fish hooks, no, instead I went for a walk in the dark forest, listening to the rustle of animals under foot and in the bush, those wild eyes darting and shooting, electric in the moonlight, and I said to myself, he is gone, it is over, I am my own woman once again...

RESOLUTIONS

Beginnings and new beginnings, and new improved beginnings, until the month of January disappears in an ending of coughs and flus, an urge for renewal, as though a beginning one month into the new year. Birthdays come and go, a celebration in party hats and ice cream cake, presents and charades, I am a father, a husband, a lover, and this weekend I see St. Valentine's Day approaching, a heart-shaped box filled with chocolates, or heart-shaped chocolates in a rectangular box, flowers in the clear glass vase, an age ago I resolved to be a better human being, a man who responded, was responsible, and if I confess, I also want forgiveness, I write this down as though a testimonial, figuring its end to be a sort of beginning, there is little more than ten months to exact these qualities, let me simplify, Oh Lord, let me be a man without television, without car, a man without a dog, one who holds no grudges, a lover man, Amen.

MOONRISE

What I say and do ("How are you?" for instance, and walk away), is not like what I think or feel (What would it be like entangled in her hair, full of heat beside her? I thought). February light descends, clear like, what? like your eyes, I say, but only to myself. Come to a celebration of your life! I'll prepare mixed drinks of exotic fruits with rum; I'll make a plate of crackers and cheese. But, here, listen to this: this is probably all it will be. Words, their sounds. This is where say is do; and do is think or feel. Dewar's on the rocks. Say it, the moon rises, and the sun sets. Moonrise; sunset. Think of a tropical place, under palms, under wraps, under cover. That's part of the formula as well. What the hell. I'll tell you another thing. I'll tell you many other things. How deeply this weather soaks into us. What is it? That is why I asked you here. Here, I mean. Right at this spot. Don't let the darkness fool you. Balloons, I have balloons. It is a fool's ball. I used to play football. Now I dance. I'll turn on the radio. Slow music.

MY NEW FLAME

I say your name, I see you, it is like a song, bell-like, I hear your voice, that is love, I touch you, I touch the moon. Fresh laundry, a new book, the smell of a baby, the smell of wildflowers, fresh on the mantel, different than anything, different than a locker room, the funk and sweat, I love the smell of the room after making love, Stevie Wonder, Duke Ellington, I still love Thelonious Monk—what the hell, and you did not say anything, looking at me, and I said, love—but forever, not so long ago, and the day was bright, in each other's arms, kissing, there we were, hopping off the page, and this drama came out of it, I love that time I wrote a line and you wrote a line. When I think of his dancers I am in love. Matisse, I wish I could paint with his simple clarity and colors, God, but then I think of a sailboat painting by Milton Avery. Who are you to tell anyone anything? Because, I say, a big liar, a hollow shell, though sometimes I feel burnt out, sometimes I even love teaching, I love experiments in prose. I still think Hubert Selby is the greatest American novelist ever. Robert Creeley. James Wright. William Carlos Williams. Wallace Stevens. I still love reading poetry. I used to love bicycles but it's been years since I've gone for a ride and used to love running but I can't now because of my back. I like anti-establishment patriots (Korean War/Vietnam War). Bottles of beer and whiskey on the table along with spicy foods. Sitting in an Asian drinking house. Flying on a 747 bound for the Orient. The rocky shoreline of Maine. The purple heather on Cape Cod. Winter or summer. The dizzy sun at the seashore. I like the way winter light—slants. Or let's pretend to be secret agents. In the late afternoon, I like to have a drink in a bar. Sitting alone. Talking to a friend. Stare out the window in the late afternoon. I love sitting in this bar on upper Broadway. Hi, mom! Hi, dad! Hi, brothers and sisters, here and in Heaven and wherever! Florida maybe. Being Irish most Irish never liked me and I feel the same. I'm into Italian and Puerto Rican culture. I'm into all of DeNiro's movies. Even if he is lazy and fat and getting over the hill, I'm still a fan of Marlon Brando, what? And I love watching Buster Keaton. Off-Broadway. Or Robert Mitchum. It

16

is an acquired taste like tobacco and liquor. Though I didn't always feel that way. I love the theatre. Get dressed. Shave. Shower and maybe take an hour. Rest afterward. That is good. I'd drink an icy beer. Played paddleball until I thought my kneecaps would fall off and my chest was pounding. I used to love the summer in the park. To play basketball and paddleball. To watch boxing. Spicy turnips. Flaming meat. Hot soups. Kimchee. I eat Korean food. When I'm not worried about my asshole. I'm not into Chinese food recently. Squid from Ideal. Coffee from La Rosita de Broadway. Cigarettes. Sushi seafood. Trying to remember what I love. About two in the morning. I sat in the park at night. A madman. Lunatic. Went into the cold street all alone. Then the other. I got it from one. Talk about love sickness? Oh boy. Found myself in love with this woman and sleeping with this other woman I loved. Love? Hah? Ha! Huh? Ah! Once I loved one person at a time. No harm done. I just like you. Okay, okay. And you go. Only some people don't like you talking like that. That is love. But I mean you. I say, love. The lights low, a quiet woman. The music soft. A quiet room. I love quiet. The lights low. The music soft. On a freezing night, but only in winter, I like it. Bushmill's Irish whiskey. And now he's on a farm in New Jersey, my bull terrier, it used to be I'd take my dog, a weekend, the promenade, or I'd go for a walk in the park. Julio done been playing around with his sweetheart Maria! The fights in the alley. The Latin lover. Green light. Red light. Its typical pulse. The city. The Bronx. Sometimes I even love. Especially around Arthur Avenue in the Bronx. Italian food. And making love in the afternoon. Let's say in the Village. I love the gray light in a hotel room. Jackie Wilson, Jimmy Reed, Van Morrison. Lips that need to be kissed. Dark eyes, black hair...

BIRTH

Born in Washington, D.C., dropped beyond the cusp of Pisces, I was reborn, in keeping with family customs, in Brooklyn six months later. Not that my brothers, oh there were many brothers, almost too many of them, nor my sisters, only a handful, or the cycle of uncles, aunts, great-relatives, great-great, and so on—not that they were reborn in Brooklyn (it is not the custom of our faith), yet their first births were recorded there, and I was reborn again many years later, this time on Long Island, once even in an upstate New York farmhouse in the middle of a cow-town and a winter blizzard (drugs), and years later still, in Morningside Heights, there again when my daughter was born, whooping, I danced in Broadway's snow with a bottle of cognac, born and reborn, dying, I died as many times, or more, than I was born, and living, I live my life, try to make a life of it, that is part of this equation, if not mother or wife, she was a breast in the night, to hold onto, to kiss, fondle, or a friend on another night, listening, and when I finished, she talked, birth against silence, rebirth instead of stillness, born in tryst, at a secret hour, in a faraway place, often only around the corner, whispers, to grope for the cord into a new light, born in dreams where only sex and death dictate the program, and waking, confusing but willing, I knock at the strange door, announcing that I am here for another birth...

JEEP

You bought a Jeep to be macho, she said. Practical, I answered. Macho, she said. And I rolled with the collision, winding up with cuts and bruises and nothing else. Once a car ran me over, not in the city, Cape Cod, a Sunday morning, Wellfleet. Usually I drove my bicycle about the city. I did not learn to drive a car until I was twenty-five. I lived nearly thirty years without owning a car. Needing wheels to get to work, I took a job out of the city. A '58 Rambler station wagon. '50 Ford coupe. '55 Chevy. There are many cars I have been party to theft of. Took them for joyrides. And those without cars hotwired cars that were not theirs. My friends had cars. The relatives. I remember a '50 Oldsmobile four-door, nine children cramped into the back seat for Sunday drives either to Flatbush or East New York. An older brother's first car was a '55 pink Ford convertible. My father's first car was a '42 Ford sedan, purchased in 1952. I grew up mostly on Long Island, car country. Upstate: Vermont: To the Cape: Up to Maine: when we lived in Connecticut. Back and forth to New York. I'd put forty thousand miles on it. "This rig will last five and maybe ten more years." The engine was rebuilt by a former Yale physicist who dropped out of the academic world to become a car mechanic and he guaranteed his work. A local motorcycle hangout. From a place called People's Garage. The car was already eight years old. I bought it outside of New Haven in 1978. A faithful machine. Never failing. Indestructible. My second car was the Volvo. My first car was a beat-up Volkswagen station wagon, rusted out, a bomb, which cost a thousand dollars to buy and another thousand to maintain for one year. Satisfied, irate, vindictive. At which she drove off. And other songs she sang until I explained that all the damage was to my Volvo and her panel truck was unscathed. "I'll kick your fucking ass, you cocksucker," she said. She was a woman truckdriver, her panel truck cut me off, and she got out screaming. Jesus McNamara, nearly at the same site, gave me a fake address after our accident, claiming that his mother was dying in the nearby hospital, and I let him drive away, my fender sloshed. Jesus! "There's a terrible entry to the parkway,"

19

I said. Up the Bronx River Parkway, over the Alexander Hamilton Bridge, to the Cross Bronx Expressway, a mess (to the muse!), at most a couple of dollars, I thought of the perils of the drive from Manhattan north. I stressed the verities of four-wheel drive. We would become gypsies. Maine and beyond in the summer. The drives cross-country to learn about our land. And I romanced about trips to the country, upstate and Vermont in winter. "This is more like a truck than a car," I said. "It's like a tank really." But I persisted, just as I had done earlier in the year with the dog. The old Volvo's fine, she said, my wife, who did not want a new car. We had no money to speak of. The works. Five forward speeds, fog defroster, big off-road radial tires, AM/FM radio, two-door model, a Jeep Cherokee, I bought my first new car, and two weeks later it was trashed in an accident, when a Ryder rental truck plowed into us at a stop light...

BETWEEN ALBANY AND SYRACUSE

The old Chevy overheats, steam billows from the radiator, green antifreeze slicks up the apron of the Thruway. Later, a mechanic down the road installs a new water hose, and chews my ear off about how bad the New York Yankees are. We drink Cokes near the busted telephone and gas station office, wondering when you'll get to see your family in Rochester. The year is 1972, late winter, almost spring-like weather, only the slightest chill in the air, and the sky clear blue. I look up into the blue sky, and I see an eagle glide over, probably eyeing a fox or rabbit in the meadow or the treeline.

APRIL

The wet is not so much everywhere as it is everything. It is. I wore a rainhat of royal blue, a raincoat of navy blue, white pants and sneakers. I walk, not miles, but just a mile today, and feel like a grunt how I trudge through this wetness. All month long mushrooms grow in corners, cherry blossoms sprout, the forsythia goes yellowy berserk, the croci formulate. Green appears. Gray works the sky. Gray fills the street. People groan, walk around as though it were full moon. Since anything is possible, nothing seems unusual. It is like wetness itself, everywhere, everything, every day this month.

YOU

You're special, you got teeth, they're neat, and your eyes, they don't twinkle, they beam, cheekbones, bone marrow, heart of curds, I'm wild about your, I'm crazy over well, I'm breathless, speechless, you, you're like, like, like walking crosstown in autumn!

MAY

An anticipation of sunshine, sunlight, Sundays in the park, some day, I thought, I'll be a contender. Meanwhile, I bite my nails. I fret, not guitars, but these small details of that day's rendezvous. You perhaps drink coffee, inhale cigarettes, going through routines of similar intensity. You get heartbeats of unusual inconsistency, you pace. Light forms in the window. Birds trill incredibly. The beaker of mustard sits untouched. Books pile up in corners that were never known to exist. Listen to the shadows. They work across the floors like cartoons or daguerrotypes, they linger and go on. Sometimes I light matches. I wink at strangers as though old friends from previous wars. They wonder, they pass. You no doubt flip baseball cards against the wall, drinking in the flower scents in the room. You prevail, in other words. I am barely getting by. Not that I mope. I hope not. I try other things, like exercise to rid me of worries, or seek out counters of well-being in the merest things in the room. This ashtray is broken. This object of no account, a leg from a chair, I wonder at. When I really play with stats, I imagine elephants, imagine tantalizing swirls of incremental heaps jerking through the air. Do I worry? Should I? Pass the salt. Pass the walls of the city. Walk again. Work. Then wake up. Wake again. Go on.

HOMAGE TO JULIA WARD HOWE

After licking my four hundredth postage stamp with your red, depressed face on the other side, Oh Julia, Oh you fourteen-cent heiress, you abolitionist and feminist, author of "The Battle Hymn of the Republic," did you ever smile once? Or was life one long suffrage, emancipation, and social cause? Didn't Gridley tickle your bones once in that nearly centenary life, New York City to Boston? My own eyes have seen the glory of William Faulkner on the twenty-two cent stamp. A few years back it was Herman Melville. But, isn't it so mail-like, so male-like, that you be relegated to postcards instead of letters? Ah, but your truth keeps marching. Invitations to gallery openings, even poems on postcards, or love scratchings. The watch fires never die out in the base camps, only now instead of it being the south and our own country, it is Central America—and I'll bet a one-dollar Eugene O'Neill stamp that I'll be a long time in Hell before I see a Smedley Butler stamp, my dear. Our stamps keep marching on...

THE WEATHER

The skies are blue, the sun is out, the temperature is seventy-five degrees, and there's no humidity. (Laughs) Only kidding. Let's face it, folks, the greenhouse effect is taking its toll. Elsewhere, the freeze is on. In the breadbasket of the country, there are tornadoes, with outlying coastal areas experiencing gale-force winds and hurricanes. The tsunami which devastated Japan, killing nearly two-thirds of its population, seems to have become no more than a ripple as it moves southerly and easterly. The earthquake in China is at an end. Two days of repercussions were felt though, and in turn set off various dormant and active volcanoes around the world, including Haleakala on the island of Maui and Kilauea on the Big Island. Sorry to report but the city of Hilo is no more. Those rains in New York? Expect more of them. So far this is the forty-eighth day of torrential rain, and no end is in sight. So I advise you Manhattanites to head toward the upper floors and you outlying boroughers to build an ark. (Laughs) Only joking. Save your irate letters, those of you out there who are still watching. (Pause) Well, if you're from Buffalo, snow is nothing new. But I guess it becomes news when the snow has been falling since June, and now six months later, the drifts in downtown Buffalo are reported to be, in some places, as high as the Eiffel Tower. Speaking of the Parisian tower, it was a bolt of lightning, and, yes, it did destroy the entire structure, killing people, Parisians and ordinary Frenchmen and tourists alike, for blocks on end. It is not so much that you shouldn't leave home without your credit card, but maybe you shouldn't leave home, period. Listen to this: earthquakes annihilate nearly all of South America. Central America totally caves in to a disastrous flood in the wake of the quakes. Hailstones the size of watermelons have wreaked havoc throughout Mexico, and if you're thinking of going to Africa to escape all of this disaster, remember to avoid the famine zones in the central area of the continent, where tourists have been known to lose more than their traveler's checks. South Africa is filled with rioting amid the one hundred mile-an-hour winds and the endless rains. Kenya stinks of dead elephants drowned in the floodtides. Liberia disappeared in a tidal wave. The islands of the Azores disappeared in the rising oceans two days earlier. A dust bowl has choked nearly all of the inhabitants of Australia, and the outlying island archipelagos of Melanesia and Micronesia have all but disappeared, including Fiji, Borneo, Tahiti, and Bora Bora. And people are still talking about how the western coast of the U.S. of A. cracked apart from the mainland, drifted into the Pacific for several miles and days, then sank inelegantly to a depth that has yet to be fathomed. At least there won't be any more pollution problems in L.A. (Laughs) That's a joke, okay? (Pause) There is a travelers' advisory, and so you should avoid Mindanao except maybe for jaunts to Davao, Iligan and Gagayan de Oro. Nix to the Sulu Islands and the Cagayan Valley in north Luzon. Sri Lanka? Government and separatists are still fighting. And it still isn't kosher to spook around the Punjab, if you know what I mean. Kidnapping is still the rage in Baluchistan, and to the west, travelers are reported to be sifting through the ashes in what once was Iran. Listen, folks, if I were you, I wouldn't be taking back any radioactive rocks for souvenirs. Elsewhere: all of Tibet is closed to outsiders, and for you old Vietnam War combat vets, Cam Ranh Bay, Danang, Dalat, and the City of Uncle Ho are all enjoying one of the hottest tourist seasons in years. If you can scrape up a few bucks, it's a fun trip, if not for the whole family—you do want a few days R & R in Bangkok with the boys— then certainly a great trip for you guys with your nostalgia and fine sense of what a fun bunch of guys and gals those Viets over there can be, am I right? (Pause) Please, please, save your letters. I don't read any of them, good or bad. Now if you are to vacation this year in Southeast Asia, but decide, for whatever reason, that you don't want to tool around Hanoi in a cyclo, then there's the B tours which go only to Bangkok, a fun place, believe you me. Only, if you're going to go touring, fellas, stick to the whorehouses and the temples. Out in the boonies the drugheads and pirates and crazos are trafficking and ornery. The Golden Triangle is a definite no-no. A lot of nice Americans have been disappearing like a plate of Oreos. Malaysia? There's a lot of malaria and dengue fever going around. Stay away.

Especially you drug addicts and dope fiends. Be advised. They'll put you to death before you can light your next Thai stick. Well, that's about it. The weather pattern should remain stable throughout the night. So I guess I'll see all of you tomorrow. Weather permitting. Have a nice day, and let's see what's in the sports picture for today. Mel?

BLACK IRISH

The other day I grew a black mustache, trimmed it, and walked out into the night like a gigolo, my hair anointed with pomade to make it slick and black like a crow. God, I am a moody gentleman, my silences like great fists and my banter like poetry. I am a father and a husband who despises all fathers, and the only good from a husband comes from his wife or daughters, voices in the wind or singing arias from the parlor. What a life I have! The other evening I strolled out, stopping at every intersection, demanding the daughters and the wives follow me like a piper, wooing them in my black cape, black hat and black scarf, black pants and shoes, like a character in a Russian play, I tell them I am in mourning for my life, and they swoon. By daylight I pass myself off as a gypsy, offering to fix pots and pans, do bodywork on their cars, or read their palms, I tinker with herbs to cure backache and pain, lost chances, or the sorrow of a lifetime, sometimes I interpret dreams or obscure texts for them, or write long testimonials. I regale the young ones in red shoes and sleek dresses with stories of the Armada, the rocky shores of the Irish coast, but then I fall quiet, slinking off into a corner of these dark rooms, brooding and smoking cigarettes. They ask me to go on, and I say I can't go on. They plead with me, knowing I'll never speak of Spaniard gold stolen, every throat cut, every corpse left to rot on the beach except for one noble captain, the swarthy Francisco de Cuellar, and though I never say it, I let them imagine the captain looking like myself when I wear the long black cape, pacing at surf's edge, full of my questions. I tell the young ones in their leopard skin blouses and their pillbox hats, the spiked heels and tiny-waisted, the ones with Italian grandmothers, I tell them how de Cuellar had a life taking him to the corners of hell, with his torments. The young ones in their party coats of soft leather ply me with sherry and port wine, and I take them inside my black cape, saying, your beauty strikes me dumb, and I never smiled until your dark eyes rested so gently on me....

FLAT-DOWN, HARD-NOSED

Wanted a hummingbird to break from my mouth, not these rat-tlesnake moans, these tin can hollers, I sing for you, let it be war-bled on-key, a juxtaposition of melody, tone, throttled grunts, reverbed burpings, chortles whimpered, pulings melliflously hammered into the threnody, what? Say what? You want to step outside and repeat what you just said to my wife, buddy? Came out flat-down, hard-nosed, squeaky or harsh, only I knew of song there, bashed symphony in the midst of the roar. Here, I bring you whistling of midnight, smoke wheeze, waddy pools, bourbon-colored, flying into the confluences like jets. The muse never begged for sonority, its appointments were breakneck, humped on scales, do-re-mi, colored by the bone-grind, meat-lust, sawdust on the dancehall floor, yodels in the back seat, bark, meow, shout, engine flywheel busted loose, the orchestra of illusions delved into the partite, the fancy handiwork of the drummer...

AN ALPHABET

In places of the world some letters are forbidden, so that alphabets contain blanked out spots on the pages, as though a censor found nothing so offensive as the act of composition, although I have heard it said that these letters were scented, that they record not so much what was done as what one wished had been done, or that she wished for the gesture to become act, and he encouraged her fancy with his own responses, thrusting his letter into the mailbox, waiting, waiting, for her answer. It was years ago, she confesses, but the old itch made words possible, and a deleted alphabet can be scented into totality. Read these words as though spoken in a whisper...

SONNET

Cat yeow, can't sleep, get up, pace the pre-aurora floor, cat black night, this kit ticked brown and black and peach, can't reach up to the sky, no moon for light, can't type, others asleep, the girl dreams of cats, her mother sleeps on her side, I'm bushed, too, eyes open, make coffee, slurp, smoke, read...

HASSLES

Life, it's a bitch, hassles at work, on the mass transit, hassles, old man arguing with bus driver, driver screaming at teenagers, you hassle me, I hassle you, the subway no better, broken down north of here, what a hassle, cold wind off the Harlem River licks your cheek raw, city life eats it, and after another hassle with the conductor and some kids about the doors, this old drunk sings: When you're smiling, when you're smiling, the whole world smiles at you, and him with that crazy grin...

PASTORAL FUNK

The problem is not the country or the people there, not their shindigs, their beer blasts or their simulated war games on abandoned acreage, nor the guns they keep in cars, in houses, on their persons, their snowmobiles or campers, the chain saws and mobile homes. It is not their four-wheel drives, not their quaint sayings like, "I'll blow the sucker away before he can say boo." No, it is not really the people in the country, but I am sick of I know not what, house weary maybe or gloomy with spring, whelmed by autumn's colors, spiked by winter's bite, or bored to tears with life. It is not the people in the country I am leaving, but the country itself, because my head wants murder, my fists, my gritted teeth, the click of my life like a well-oiled knife, the beat, the shuffle, gridlock and stalled shuttles, crammed buses, the cry of the heated cat in the night, homeless women with no teeth, homicide and rape, the wonders of fashion in alleys, how the men on street corners whistle at the passing strangers, all women, grease on their tongues, how the men on corners whistle. It is not the country or people in the country, but my nervous fingers, my bony wrists, my nervous ganglia, my hypertensions that call me back to the city...

MONOLOGUE OF A MANIAC

Why I was shouting at you, I was drunk, incoherent, so what? My tongue suffers if I cannot murder silence, and my words flow from jisms of, hell, can I say neglect without sounding droopy corny sappy stupid? I am intoxicated by the mundane and spectacular. I'm a nice guy! I'm not shouting! I am not shouting! WHO'S SHOUTING? Rivers of plurals, mounds of nouns, they needed some kind of release. I accompany them on such journeys, sort of like an unpaid amateur guide into the voids of neurotic snits and fits and shiteating grins. Sing to me, talk me to sleep, let's turn the page. Ah, fuck you, too! AND I'M NOT SHOUTING!

LA RONDA

And I am drunk on Friday night my brother Joe is drunk so we go around the corner to La Ronda where no one speaks English and the go-go girl is Dominican she shakes her booty and Oh my wife is angry with me because I am drunk and my brother Joe is also drunk and together we have come for more drinks at La Ronda and to watch the go-go girl go-go her sequins shake around and around they go-go Oh my and her breasts are lovely brown and shaped like coconuts but not hairy like a coconut they look soft like mango but shaped like coconuts Oh I am drunk my brother and my wife is mad but the go-go dancer smiles and dances her head off like there was no tomorrow Oh I am drunk and my brother I can't remember which brother it is I am with but he is drunk as usually most of my brothers are on the weekend and if they were in La Ronda with me they would be drunk too Oh he is drunk my brother and I am drunk and even the go-go dancer is drunk it is that late in the evening and we watch her dance the go-go on Friday night at La Ronda and...

MADE IN THE USA

Because the horses were tired and so were your feet, because we were hungry, because of sweat, of thirst, of a need to communicate across great distances, we invented. Because we are a land of inventors, not imitators, not refiners, we're discoverers, we invented red meat, Twinkies, underarm deodorant, aerosol sprays, nickel beer (two bucks with inflation). The telephone rings, digital time pulses, instantly the coffee is made, instantly one becomes famous. Hollywood, movies, the invention of television, the eight-hour day, the fifty-minute hour, one-hour dry cleaning that takes a week if you don't get it in before nine in the morning. Because a pig foot and a bottle of beer was too much to take, you made peanut butter and jelly sandwiches on Wonderbread: Rock & Roll! Rock & Roll! Rock & Roll!

THE SQUIRRELS

Don't be fooled by their cuteness, really they are rats in mottled furs. Examine their teeth sharp as blades, their claws like longshoremen's spikes. They are not nice, either. Hoot at them, holler, stamp your foot—watch them leap! There is a black one I see on the way to work, always foraging in the dry leaves, and it reminds me of the devil or Holy Ghost, I run for it, scared to death, through the parking lot, up the stairs, and into my office, I lock the door, and on my knees, praying in a whisper, I offer an imprecation, another unholy prayer…

THE MARTYR

Ashes fell into my primavera sauce, leave it, I said, let me experience the pasta a la Assisi, and afterward I picked up a hairshirt, joking, I threw off my cotton one, and said, let me see how this feels. We walked miles and miles on a narrow road upward into the hills until our feet blistered, and then you noticed I wore no shoes, it was snowing, blood on the trail, my footprint like the spoor of a wounded animal. I tried to quell her alarm, kidding that I forgot to wear my shoes, so what? The next thing you'll be looking at my hands for the signs of stigmata. We looked at my chilblained hands, then pretended none of this happened...

DEER WILDCAT FOX DOG

I shot at the deer with my bow and arrow, letting the head of the quivered arrow puncture its heart, and then I went out into the snow, following the bloodtrail. In the bare woods I came upon a wildcat, sleek as a dancer, baring its teeth, its nipples swollen with milk, and when I kneeled to taste its urine, the cat bolted away because it was in heat and knew that I knew the story. I walked along the saddle of a hill of evergreens, still following the bloodtrail from the wounded deer, and saw a fox as slick as a shaman, tricked out in the burnt colors of the season, it snarled at me, then darted off like a naked woman discovered at her bath. But the bloodtrail finally ended near a well, and I walked back into the woods, empty-handed, until I heard a woman sigh, a man pant, and I stole up to the place where the naked woman lay in a pile of straw, the man on top of her, and she wept for him not to take her handkerchief, and pleaded with him not to make her big dog bark. I came back along the snowy trail to where I had set up my camp, lit a new fire, ate a meatless dinner, and then wrote all these ordinary events of my day into a notebook…

ALMOST NEARLY MID-LIFE
BREAKDOWN BLUES

I grow fat on the rump and in the waist I expand, my hair grows thin and gray. Hey, I feel shab, a drear, old fangled and near flinty, ox-like I reply to flirts, don't call me dear. Consider my wallet: photos of gone dog, of child in stages and wife on rock, I.D., Chinese laundry ticket, wad of singles, married now, soon-to-be out of work, my pants are tight, buckle run out of holes, my bucket with the hole in it, my pig foot is no longer lucky, and I drink beer out of the bottle when in my cups. Once a lover, I was woman-adored, and in turn adored them back, hanging their panties over my mirror. I smelled my fingers of nicotine and fish, I walked with a strut, cock-of-the-walk, I smiled like a matinee idol, but with the teeth of a wino, and the charm of a wino, and wino breath. What a wreck! I swore like a sailor, having once been one, and like old and abandoned boats called derelicts, I was derelict in my fatherly duties, my husbandly tasks, like going out for milk, and coming back tomorrow. For years I acted as though I were twenty-one years old, then my back went, I woke up, and in the mirror was a man. He was thirty-eight years old...

A MAN

I punch my fist into the dirt, making a crater the size of a human face, and throw dumb seeds into the hole, full of my hopes. I kick down trees rotted through the long winter from ice and snow, I rip stumps from the sodden ground and throw them a hundred yards down the road. I squeeze the shrubs and bushes, pinching them, I mutter, grow you dead dumb bastards and roots, bud and bring some life into this valley, run and burst, burst and grow. I lie back in the shade, and listen to them burst and grow, I hear their colors forming in the ground from the mulched earth and rain, I smell their tensions and shapes.

THE IRIS (ii)

The purple sword-leaft flower droops in the early May heat as day threatens a rain never to come and I thought of another kind of iris, the circular diaphragm forming the color of eyes. This is how photographs become artful or a man sees a woman and wishes he had his camera as the wind raises up her skirt, her eyes flash, she whirls around by the iris plantings, searching for the light, and he wishes, he wishes he had his camera…

THE CIRCUMFERENCE
OF MY CIRCUMSTANCE

Certain rules of order must be followed, even in the terrible circumstance of living one day to the next, so if the day is bright, light matches, and when it is dark, close your eyes. Pour water on your head, when it rains, and carry a hot water bottle inside your pants during the dog days of summer. If it freezes, fill your pockets with ice cubes, and pray for snowdrifts. If this is life, then call it that, and nothing else, and if it is love, well, love, call it by the name it is given. We fight because of love, and sometimes it appears as though we love to fight, words, mostly, shoves, occasionally, though never deadly blows to the head or sneaky punches to the stomach or kidneys. The rules are followed exactly, and circumstance is accounted for: if this is love, if this is life...

AS IF

It is as it were (so be it) a rainy day, as if, i.e., I walk in teardrops,
rain drops, tumbles from the sky (Oh my!), it rains, as they say,
day after day, slops everywhere (I should care), umbrella in
hand, other hand—on the other hand—in my pocket (fuck it),
let it rain, as though (as such), that is, these drops are warm (I
mean no harm), I am reminded, again, then again, and again,
of your arm which leads to your neck, which joins your head
(lips, eyes, nose, mouth, hair, etc.), Etcetera, the rain says, drip-
drop-plop (I'm dancing), I walk in it to you, for you I get wet
(you bet), sunshine, I say, Here I am, I mean, I am here, in this
chair, and my hair is wet, my feet are wet, I have a cold (ah, you
are warm), your warm, your tender, your loving arms, I'll
change, turn it around, I'll wear dry clothes, I'll be something
or other, perhaps your lover (I butter up), button, unbutton, I
see your eyes, like a boy to a wanton, my fly, the gods (Eee-
gads!), the climate here is nothing like the weather...

LANGUAGE LASSO

If you look in the thesaurus under psoriasis, you will find a pressed wild flower from summers ago in Maine. The thing is that I was trying to spell the word brontosaurus when all of this happened...

THE NEAR-EMPTY REFRIGERATOR WITH SIX SMALL BOTTLES OF CLUB SODA

Desmond is Ruth Ellis' good friend in the movie, *Dance with a Stranger*. A bachelor, he is the one always helping her out of violent predicaments with her boyfriend, Blakely, a rich drunken playboy, with whom Ruth falls madly in love. If I was going to name an object which reminds me of Desmond, poor, sad fellow, I first would say the loyal dog you can kick around and come back to at anytime. But Desmond is not an animal; he's a gentle man, adoring of his friend who runs an after-hours pub and who looks like Marilyn Monroe, and maybe is as uncertain as the star; Ruth takes all kinds of abuse from Blakely, and every romantic encounter turns into a violent confrontation, which still she comes back to, playing it again and again. Her friend Desmond is her anchor, and yet I would not say that he reminds me of an anchor. Who is he? Towards the end of the movie, just before Ruth kills Blakely, she and her son move into Desmond's flat, and at one moment the boy opens the refrigerator to see what is there. The refrigerator is empty except for six or so small bottles of club soda, and I realized that that image is Desmond, a near-empty refrigerator with six small bottles of club soda.

A.I.R.

Grab my halcyon coat of leather and lamb's wool, my pellucid hat—I speak about one of those rare beats in my condition—I jig about the table, finger the lattice work of the walls, catch the first elevator, and I am gone. The sun is bright like a halogen lamp, the street glistens like ions. My neighbors wear bon vivant and c'est la vie in lapels, their smiles all muchas gracias. Bums in my parish fleece the passersby with to-do, the affectionate mother squeezes tomatoes, flirting with the melon of the greatest consistency. Every man and every woman is quite something today, blue in the sky, bright in the exact places, even shaded for those of such disposition. Consignments reflect mutual aid, and nearly all have jettisoned their beggarly dreams for the flamboyant utterances of local raconteurs. Even the racketeers would rather play ball than haggle. Church bells extoll, the rudiments of day filled like your ashtrays used to be with butts. The famish-ones feel like famous-ones. Old voyeurs blink as diplomats patsy around, each of them eyeing the women of fur and down, the ones of nylon and gray sweat pants, and it feels like a bra commercial the way the men and women strut. Damn the clocks, even when broken, they are right twice a day...

FORGET THE HEART

If the parts of the body be known which are affected by love, let me suggest the liver and kidneys react far more than the heart, for the giblets are abused and broken when the lover is without love, too much wine, or the waiting brings hypertension when the telephone does not ring as prescribed. The stomach is another area affected by love, how it churns with spicy food, or even consider the maladies of the asshole, hemorrhoids, etc., or pacing the room, corns and calluses affect the feet. He touches himself; she touches her clitoris. She wonders if anyone will touch it again. Will it drop off like a button whose thread has unwound? Will his penis fall off from lack of activity? Somehow the heart seems irrelevant. Think of eyes, red with tears, a running nose, a dry mouth, imagine the hands twisted and knotted, the nails bitten, the worn elbows, the belly, the buttocks, the ears. Somehow the heart does not count.

WALKING THE BRONX

1.

Where the river breaks a dogleg left, the Harlem into Hudson at Spuyten Duyvil, nightly I wait for the Broadway local after work at the 225th Street elevated, Marble Hill's pulse like guaracho or guaguanco. Earlier in the daylight of late morning, I got off the subway here, walked down the stairs, and stood at the bus stop, facing eastward up the big hill at Kingsbridge Road, rode past the Armory on Jerome, young man with piebald pit bull on a long chain, girl with Doberman, old red-faced gal with German shepherd, and a white-haired purple-nosed priest come out of a local tavern. Work finished I came down Fordham Road, looked in the window of an oriental store selling imitation Cabbage Patch dolls for ten dollars, crossed the Concourse after coming out of Poe Park, his cottage, and I think of Edgar Allan, and I tell him, Mr. Poe, Mr. Poe, the Bronx is on fire, Mr. Poe…

2. *Pastoral in Spotlights*

A beast with breasts, this beautiful monkey of a woman, high-heeled and in leather, dancing her butt off on the moonlit floor, whore and saint, the lights of faint autumn, the night of chills, dance with her in the hills in your overloaded dreams, through a field of mud and wet grass, locate your thrills, and imagine yourself her lover, this monkey painted like a rainbow turned into a woman, and dream of the beast with two backs, the act of darkness, of nature in the city, or the wind inside of buildings…

3.

Once in the Bronx I heard the poet Seamus Heaney read his work to a roomful of Jesuits and others, his sound so palpable the words did a crazy synesthesia in my brain, I smelled potatoes, not in my mother's Irish kitchen or grandma's, but of the potato fields, those truck farms that used to border our town when I was a boy growing up on Long Island, so rich it was like an aphrodisiac, and made your head spin until you reached the edge of Bloody Hollow woods or the potent flops in Cowtown north, you left the truck farmer and his potatoes in a wind moving in a different compass direction, and I smelled it again as an adult with my wife and daughter, driving on the North Fork in late summer, and again at the reading in the Bronx, and to think my father's relatives went to bed nightly, smelling of such fields, with a touch of poteen on their breaths...

4.

Listen to the gulls off the Harlem River, the night sky is purple and the wind cuts at the stillness. Our walk of three miles ended, now we depart after catching our breaths, but instead of leave-taking, we listen: the wind, the gulls, buses, the Spanish language streets, the car horns, even sounds from the river. Another time: we drank beer in an Irish bar on Fordham Road, even shots of Irish whiskey, then walked up Kingsbridge through Poe Park, and the doggerel streets, street kids and street punks, pizza, the breathlessness of the night, down the saddle of that hill near the VA hospital, across a bridge at the Major Deegan, to Broadway and 225th Street, the gulls off the Harlem, the purple night, wood smoke from a garage in the air, the waves from the river...

5. *Dancing to Salsa in Nueva York*

In my raw silk jacket and linen pants, my ears came unplugged from the tangents created by her mambo, or the papaya I drank while she pulsed exquisite tango. My feet were connected to the ankle bones, my ankle bones were connected to my calves, on up to my knee joints (dumb joints they are), my fat thighs splashed about, my belly jiggled to her crazy lacy spacy guaguanco, and my legs were alive with this spongy plosion, and the nutty spansions of feet to floor, I called out please oh please save that last dance that last dance for me...

A FIFTIES INDEPENDENCE DAY

What changed is only the cast of the day's light, working from deep sweat to cool evening breeze, and the voices of the children growing more cantankerous in the explosion of firecrackers, and their ghostly faces lit by illegal sparklers. The adults were fought-out, drunk-up, eaten full with barbecue, and another beer keg was tapped, sunset mauve, radio playing Elvis Presley and Frank Sinatra, the father announced to his male in-laws that he would still rather fight than talk, and who among them would be first to put up their dukes, and even though their heads nodded in agreement, they were fathers themselves now, and it being so dark, they reasoned, what was the point of throwing punches that could not possibly land with any accuracy? Maybe tomorrow, they said, on the Fifth of July.

SOLOMON SAYS

1.

You are fair, love, look how fair you are—you have dove's eyes in your locks, your hair is like a flock of goats, they appear on the mountain. Like a flock of sheep, your teeth, even shorn, after washing—let all twins be born, none barren. Your lips are like a thread of scarlet, of garlic, your speech handsome, your temples like a bit of pomegranate within those locks. Neck, you are like the tower of David, wherein rest a thousand bucklers for mighty men. Two breasts like two roes, let them feed among the lilies. From night to daybreak, let me get to the mountain of myrrh, to the hill of frankincense, to the ginger inside of your thighs. You are fair, love, there is no spot on you. Come with me from Lebanon, spouse, and from the lion's den, from the leopard's mountain...

2.

You ravish my heart, sister, spouse, your eye ravishes me. Your neck ravishes me. Your vagina is like a cup of honey. How fair is your love, sister, spouse! Better than wine, and the smell of your ointments is better than spices or strong beer. Your lips, spouse, drop as the honeycomb—honey and milk under your tongue, the smell of your garments is like the smell of Lebanon. A garden enclosed, that is you. Eucalyptus on the hill. A spring shut up, a fountain sealed. Your plants are an orchard of pomegranates, such pleasant fruits. Camphire, with spikenard, spikenard and saffron, calamus and cinnamon, with trees of frankincense, myrrh and aloes, with all chief spices. A fountain of gardens, a well of living waters, a stream from Lebanon, an oasis in the desert, a palm shade from the heat. Awake, O north wind, come south, blow upon my garden that these spices may flow out, and let my love come into this garden, and let my love eat these pleasant fruits...

UNIONIZING THE ONION FACTORY

Management refused to give in in the early stages of negotiations when the workers demanded handkerchiefs or sprigs of parsley near the water cooler and the washrooms filled with lemon oil, but ten thousand workers, crying, in the Square of Onions with a background of old world onion-domed structures, made the entrepreneurs take notice, grown men, red-faced women in their babushkas, the children's knotted hands deformed from hours of peeling without unionized standards, o those bloody capitalists were not immune to their tears, or how the workers' skin peeled away layer on layer until nothing was left but the heap of pulp on the sawdust floor. Management's flacks claimed to be unmoved, unwitting, intractable, about the cost of living increases, retirement schedules, pensions, health plans, and even though few died of heart attacks in the factory, an inordinate number of workers lived with broken nasal passages —a coincidence, the bosses claimed—or the high incidence of blurred vision, not to mention the social ostracism some of the workers felt in their communities, or how few of them were able to eat bland food. The workers' claims were not unreasonable, they were just, and when ten thousand of them sat down at their peelers and mincers, their dicers and shredders, the enormous silence was enough to solidify their cause, they were brothers and sisters in a fight to obtain parity, and their banners draped from the windows of the onion factory: DOWN WITH ONION SOUP! UP WITH THE PEOPLE! Or that photograph of the child in swaddling clothes, a large placard draped over its stroller: MAN DOES NOT LIVE BY ONIONS ALONE! UNIONIZE TODAY! First they brought in tear gas, but it proved worthless. We hurled onions at the police. Then they used water cannons, injuring many of us, and locking out our union supervisors. Massive rioting followed, and these wounds will not heal...

GIANT

The mimosa tree is green and pink at a distance; close up its blossom is bushy purple and yellow. Bees plunder the nectar, zero in on blossom, drink. My daughter wants to touch the leaves which are green and ferny; she demands I bend the bough, releasing that pungent orchid into her hands. I'm being reasonable, adult, the caring father; I say, look at it and enjoy it. We don't want to destroy this wonderful tree, it only blossoms this time of summer, and soon it will be green, and the blossoms gone. I've got a friend named Giant, she says, and he's bigger than these buildings, as big as the sky. And he's going to rip this tree out of the ground with his hands, and put it in a cage for me. He's going to keep the bees away, and I won't get stung; he's going to make these flowers purple and yellow all year round. He's tough, and bee bites will only feel like mosquitoes; he won't cry. Giant will let me pick all the 'mosa blossoms I want; he's not my father, she says.

CROW FATHER

Pick up a feather crow it looks like fallen from the big pines they come through here like a pack of airships or Cobras filled to the gills with early scavenger raids some crow as big as a man in their wing spans they spin in the wind like drunken fathers or like father like son like the crow itself...

EDINBURGH SKETCHES

Kells

These Celtic squares in the dreary light of rain around these Scottish streets and closes and gardens, as though Deacon Brody were around the corner with his sack filled with living and breathing things, and Mr. Hyde bolted out on cue in his madman's outfit, bowling over an errant child, all beauty and the beast. I buy a silk scarf for the woman from a country gal who made it, and notice the pattern is from the Book of Kells with its eight circle cross. "Found in the Gospel," the old one tells me from behind her stall in the basement of a churchyard beside the blackstoned church in the shadow of the castle on the hill, and the pipers wailing. "According to Saint Matthew," she says, referring to the pattern of the circles, and I leave the crafts fair into the rain and go down the Lothian Road to the bed and breakfast place, but stop first for a few gills or a pint of heavy at Bennett's. I examine the scarf at the bar, its eight circle cross, and the silkiness of its silk, lavender and gold, pondering the circles that are really squares...

Alba

This was in the cloudy moonlight of that medieval city in a summer filled with rain and cold nights, where I bought dinner, and later walked your dog. This was in August when the rain stopped momentarily and the street lights were out, and the sounds of the night everywhere, as though I walked in bare feet through the street of this Lothian romance. Back in your wee bit of a room, we drank off the rest of the booze, until the sun rose, the room lightened, and with the day come I had to catch the train, and I said, I'll send flowers, but instead wrote this alba...

Christina's Sestina

The cloud scud in the sky is illuminated by the full moon at midnight, even without the wind. Dog bark, footsteps, rainfall, over the cobbles, running the street with small rivers of black water. I don't like the taste of the water in this city, and so drink in the sky, watching out not to trip in the street, although there is a light from the moon. Now it is silent except for rainfall over the cobbles, and there is no wind. There is rain, but there is no wind. The black street runs with black water, and you say to be careful not to fall in this dark close with a sliver of sky at its peak, and I say that the moon is bright enough in the night sky to protect us from a great fall. If you listen carefully to the water fall on the cobbles, overrunning the street and pouring down from the night sky, you forget to hear the howling wind (newly arrived), and listen to the water music, the cloud break, and the moon. I do not care for the ways of the moon, I said, watching the black water fall over the sidewalk, the silly water music of leaves filling the dark street, black water and the talking of the wind, and clouds scudding in the dark sky. The moon vanishes from the late sky, and the rain diminishes, the wind falls off, water stops running in the street…

SWAMP WILLOWS OFF A TURNPIKE

This highway of weeds, swamp willows, marsh orchids, bed-springs and beer cans, the wind your only companion, but hear the roar of the turnpike distantly as if it were a dream, and see how big the sky is, a dome, a blue egg, a well that is upside down, and you are diving, falling, gone into the swamp again...

MAN IN A STREAM

The ugly stick beats the air like a pendulum, the wrist snaps into an arc, spool unravels yards of eight-pound test up the leads on the graphite rod, a Shakespeare, the handmade fly iridesces on the dance of the current, it beckons trout from the stalker in wading boots, porkpie hat, willow creel slung on shoulder, his many-pocketed vest filled with gadgets to trick the fish out of their patterns in the stream. And in better times, and days, the death of urban man was thought to be this incarnation...

HOUSES

I.

You build a house of wood and white stone, facing a sunset off the pond, I thought you might make it of your plans, our delicate relationship, disregarding the ordinary designs of men and women, let the patterns form organically, a house of cabbages, onions, garlic, or a house of breath and heat, an ondol floor, and without secret doors, and no closets because in the garden of first light, everyone walks naked or bathes in communal tubs, except for the spiral stairs leading to secret towers, where meat and fish are grilled on open fires, scallions and hot pepper sauce. It is indelicate of me to talk houses with you; we should not talk of houses, but how you are and I am well. Yet this idea of ideals, of you and houses that we share, related as we are by this interest in habitats, and the habits of men and women in them, a house formed as it were without nails, joined by fitting one part into quite another part...

II.

In the pasture I'd manure, I'd dump shit to make the earth grow like crazy, I'm crazy, you understand, about you and your houses, I'd ask for monuments, something like an obelisk. I'd call for a squared circle, demanding impossible things, I'd yawp about the traditions, the law, and human instincts, I'd hem about, I'd haw over the hen house, I'm a man, I'd yell, and so would speak of procedures, I would, claiming I never felt this way about you until you felt this way about houses, since we are speaking of them, I would speak of these houses with you, I'd talk and talk about them, and maybe you would speak, about houses or the garden and the fields, the late afternoon sunlight cutting across the opaque windows at the pavilion near the stream, and the view to the woods where wild deer run...

III.

A house speaks, or maybe I am listening, it settles, or its inhabitants vacate, it is empty, and so hollow, like the inside of a knot-
hole, a cave as ancient as fire, each room echoes a voice, this is
why I like houses, they communicate when we are silent, and
this is not my home, I live in another city, and you live down
the road, let's drive back, these rooms are full of ideas, and I am
taken by the wood, or maybe the idea of wood, and you are
interested in other kinds of design, I understand, a house is like
that, so many textures, grooves and circles, angles, I like angles,
and its shadows are as important as the light it draws in...

IN SEARCH OF THE SILK ROAD

I grew up in Brooklyn and still remember the row of brownstones in East New York until one day my parents bagged us—not ten or fifteen, only five children back then—into the back seat of my uncle's new Packard, and went east out to Long Island. There hollyhock and lilac grew, giant sumac and barky sycamores, a white birch, dogwood, sandy roads, and woods only a quarter of a mile in any direction. The fishman came every Friday in his Ford Model T Woody, and low tide at the beach smelled like dirty underpants. My brothers stole horses to ride in that meadow across the railroad tracks behind the old butcher shop, and sometimes I went with a classmate to Cowtown, and she or he threw rocks at the pastured cows. There was a sandpit, bottomless, they said, which led all the way to China...

THE END OF DAYLIGHT SAVING'S TIME

1.

If you listen, the leaves glide to their own music, and you taste
the air's fever as though it were a hot pepper. Here, I am color-
blinded by the frenzy of reds in the poison ivy or the sapped
yellows of oak and elms. If you touch the ground, the ground
responds, its crust opens, it breathes. If you touch, the earth
whispers, Touch me again, and again you touch. Stay in touch,
one writes in a letter scented like a flower burst open in its own
heat, and the scent of the letter is like a hand on your face...

2.

The perfume of spring fades into summer's funk as it sweats
and coils into the deeper months of the year, September into the
feast of St. Francis, the sound of leaves spins noisily like rockets,
they land like insects on old meat, they thud on the path like
bricks. The promenade is strewn with red, cardinal and papal
scarlet, lamb's blood, and there are rainbows shot from the veins
of the fallen elm leaves, and you hear the tree sap jerk down
into the big roots of the giant black oaks and the ancient maples,
branches crack in testy winds. On an obscure path, in the
absence of dogs and humans, you touch everything in sight,
leaf, stone, branch, imagining them fingers or bones, eyelids and
earlobes. You breathe with the new breath of evening, clear and
cold, haughty, and alone. If you danced, it would be compli-
cated by the knowledge of your old desires, and these newer
urges to shout the names of the living in this declining land-
scape.

HANGDOG EXPRESSION

I dream I am George Patton again, only my bull terrier is smaller, and brindled, but then the dream change works, and I send the dog to Jersey, with that fireman with the Toyota jeep and the big mustache, the shoulders like a bulldozer, telling me about a house of pit bulls and fifteen cats. Even if the dog bit Mora twice in one summer, shat on the rug innumerable times, and ate an entire football, he was not without his grace and charm. I have to ask myself, what can you say about a man who sends his dog away?

FOOTBALL

The cornerback told me to blitz from my middle linebacker spot, pump, strut, I smiled, happy to oblige him, full of confidence about sacking the quarterback, I pumped my legs, flapped my arms, and rushed up the slot, knocking the kid on his sorry ass. My wife shook me awake from the bliss of sleep, 5:30 AM, and asked what kind of crazy sex dream I was having. Youth, I said, a boyhood dream, you wouldn't understand, and she didn't, when I explained it a few hours later over coffee...

IMITATED FROM YEATS'
"IMITATED FROM THE JAPANESE"

This is quite amazing—I have lived forty-four years! (Let's hear it for the bare trees in fall, for fall is here already.) Forty-four years I've lived, no longer ragtag, hangdog, forty-four years, nearly all a boy but now a man, and if I dance, I dance because I kissed her, and I kissed her because I am a man, and this woman makes me dance!

THE MAD MAN

There sits a man, a mad man, he jumped bail, he bounced checks, and fled to South America by plane, where the plane was hijacked, and the heat was on, he wound up in Corsica, he journeyed to Egypt, to Syria, into the turmoil of Lebanon, freed, he went to Southeast Asia, worked the harvests of the Golden Triangle, fell in love, went straight, moved to a good street, raising a family of fourteen children, and when this brood was grown, he came home to the city, he lived to an old age, dying on his birthday, and now the story of him is all bones...

MEMORY AND DOUBT

Was all childhood this nut of pain? How was I to remember it? This vague harking backward is like an itch. To remember. To forget. Much of what is is formed from what was that first compulsion—a recollection of long nights in that house. Ivy. Sumac. Oak. All poisons. Yellow stucco walls on which to scrape your new skin. I doubt I really remember…

ENEMIES: A TRIPTYCH
WITH BROKEN MIRRORS

1.

A perfectly friendly one who laughed at all your gossip and jokes—it is hard to believe him out there playing Iago now—better as children we badmouthed each other, only to be friends by nightfall—now the stakes are higher, or less, but a knife in the back, these cutthroats in ascots, blame it on the state of the arts, or let them talk behind your back, of good ones and bad ones, and even in your goodness, let find your faults, laugh at it, don't be paranoid, don't carry a gun wherever you go, and be ready to use it at the slightest provocation, the slightest annoyance, or possiblity they may talk, shoot them dead, or challenge them to a duel at the break of dawn. Whiplash of tongues. Magpie chatter. Their feeble observations. This is its own violence. Pace off ten steps. Using swords or lugers, choose a dramatic setting like Central Park, and have your seconds available to chamber the bullets in the pearl-handled revolvers your Uncle Leo used to shoot his neighbor half a century ago, and wear shoes that won't mind the dew, and don't smoke before, because it suggests one about to smoke his last cigarette, but do allow your enemy to smoke, also hinting that it is *his* last, then take your positions in the field—observe the angle of sunlight, how shrewd you are to choose the east, and don't allow your hand to shake, steady it, firm it, and be ready to give this ass his due, and yet just before you pull the trigger, you ask why he plays Iago to your, what? The pistols fire, one of you falls…

2.

As children we badmouthed forever—were friends by nightfall—now the stakes are higher, or less—the knife cuts, the cutthroats mingle—come, let me freshen your drink, let me read your next book—the tongue is violent too—oh, Iago, you never respected the code of silence…

3.

One who laughed—perfectly reassuring in the intimacy of his glance, and how he gulled you into his confidence—or how that other went hot and cold depending on his barometer of your social importance. There was the female Iago, too, her breeches' role that made her imagine herself some kind of Sarah Bernhardt of betrayals, or maybe a Vanessa Redgrave. Or the epicene one who played his part like a fool at the gallows. Some of their violations were downright elegant. When they talk, they talk of you. Don't be paranoid. Even as you are informed of this, they are off somewhere saying perfectly nasty things, both true and untrue. They wear sneakers or loafers, jeans, sweatsuits, jumpers, seersucker. Doesn't it gall you? It is so intransigent of them, having judged you forever that way, and all you did was tell one his wine stunk, the colors of another's suit clashed with the wallpaper, say to a third that orange socks were not classy or fashionable, and to a fourth that intelligence was not what she was claiming it was—how many bodies, male and female, she slept with in a month. Really, it is enough to make you laugh!

TRACT

After reaming the frontier, we adjourned for glasses of port. (I say "we," but nearly everyone knows I did these deeds alone.) The world was skewered, the rich drank beer and complained of holes in their socks, while the poor dreamed of white Cadillacs. (I say "the rich," but I mean the middle class, and "the poor" were an entity in some official's mind during his last re-election.) I voted to occlude outer space, and my candidate won his election fists down. ("This" is a worthless attempt at a political tract, yes?) I opt for pornography, a good whore's story: lingerie, nipples, fertile thigh, scent of musk, dripping honeycombs and petards, friction of body heat under klieg lights. Ah. Ah. That's better!

MYTHS OF CREATION

But I remember my parents like they were Uranus and Ge. Children popped from mother, each nine-month cycle brought forth a new brood. We were children born of a presumptuous father, as though he were the first to devise shameful action. I always thought him capable, in his animal fertility, of stuffing each one of us back into the motherhold. And mother telling us his great insolence had to be punished with the sickle she fashioned from gray adamant. And so we made revolutions. Like Cronus, I undertook to accomplish the deed, since I did not care for the abominable father. I took the jagged-tooth sickle, lying in ambush for him. And home from his labors, I cut off his genitals, flung them out the window, and an ash tree sprung. From the bloody drops, carried off on the sea swell of ocean, white foam of bloody flesh, another girl was born, a dread and beautiful child. Washed by the waves, they called her Aphrodite, genital-loving Philomedes, wholly formed from his genitals. Eros attended her; desire followed her. And from these scars, I father, I roar through the heavens. That I am Cronus, Father of Zeus, Father of Poseidon, Father of Demeter, Father of Hera, Father of Hestia. And like my own father, I devour children. The moment they pop from the bloody womb, I eat them as though they were gods. My wife wrapped stones in infant clothing, telling me of another child. My belly fills with stones. I am not the ruler of immortals...

THE RUNAWAY

In my dreams of want, I wrote poems in the gas station on Hillside Avenue where I worked every weekend into late night just before I turned fifteen years old. I talked with the punks who came by, working on their Harleys, and kept the beer cold inside the Coke machine. When I was fifteen, I ran away from home to the Village, where I holed up in four-fifty a night SRO hotels, drinking sweet wine and writing in my notebooks. Every morning I attended mass at St. Anthony of Padua on Sullivan Street, still a practicing Catholic. Afterward, I'd drink Italian coffee, eat a roll, and read until the early afternoon. I walked everywhere downtown, from Fourteenth Street down to the Battery and back, and, really screwed up one day, I stopped into this church on the Lower East Side, imagining the Blue Virgin dripping tears, until I took a subway out to Queens and then a bus to my family's house on Long Island...

NOVEMBER

You see the cold and smell it before it kisses you, there, and I want to walk on dead leaves, maybe even climb a mountain. Winter is only an hour's drive north, let's go, I'll make sandwiches of peanut butter, you brew some barley tea, and we'll drive up to and into the country. The heater in the jeep is raised high, the sky stone gray. Here, wear this scarf, and take my gloves. There. We are ready to go...

SUNDAY SONNET

The windows open to the weather, November breezes into the south room, sun streams, cat fur, dust dances through the lavender curtains. Goddamn the man, and the woman and the child, I sing in my rooms, damn him, for it is Sunday, and therefore I sing these curses in bone-white rooms of late morning orange juice and rolls, of smoked salmon and smelt. Since this is the sabbath, I take my bath, I read the funnies, I wait for football games to begin. Instead of gin, I drink a cold beer…

READING APOLLINAIRE
AFTER TOO MANY BEERS

The anemone and the ankle are poised against the garden wall asleep melancholy between love and deodorant. If I come again with these hombres can you not despair. The soles of our feet are rent sombreros with all that disparity. The diets of old wives lazy cool in their Chevies parked in front near the poor Swedes one beautiful hombre has your eyes...

A COUPLE IS A PAIR

Tender person, oh lady of genius, generous and tender, coupling, uncoupling, forever in tempests, you are no temptress, trusty mate. All this gender, engendering, generating heat and trust, simply because we met, and therefore we lusted. It was a couple of people, meeting, then pairing—I am not comparing that to now—but like then, we were a couple engendering, your gender breaking across my gender, and I was tender, you were too...

WAR

Kelly tells a war story. He sits in the backroom of that sleazo bar up the block on Broadway. He belts down beers, everyone full of rear echelon sympathies. The day bartender is gone, himself a wounded and dressed and decorated veteran of the Korean War. "Was east of Plei Boi," Kelly says, "north of Mo Phuc, what they called Firebase Bleeding Jesus, formerly LZ Jesus, Mary, & Joe..." He downs his beer and waves for another. Salerno sits in one of the darker corners of the table, his eyes invisible in this light. "Where?" Salerno asks flat out. You see, Salerno caught some heavy shit in Eye Corps near the ville of Suc Roc, and a combat vet, he cannot make out the geography of Kelly's tale. "The Highlands," Kelly answers, too indifferently. "Hmmm," Salerno goes, like he tasted a rancid fish sauce. The young bloods at the table take both men in, savoring their words and wishing one day themselves to be tending bar out front or sitting back here at these tables, shadows playing across their blank killer eyes, wrinkles in their faces, wounds maybe healed up and pulsing like little heartbeats on their backs and shoulders. Sonya is the only woman at the table, really a girl, a young woman, and she leans into the light to address handsome Kelly. "Somebody said you had fourteen brothers and sisters," she says, but says it as though asking a question. "Twelve," Kelly says, and drinks off half his bottle of new beer. "You told me ten the other day," Salerno says. Kelly laughs as Salerno scowls. "Big family," Kelly says, smacking his lips. "How many were there?" Salerno wants to know. "Were there?" Kelly asks. "Or are there? It's a big difference, Sally." "Either fucking way," Salerno says. "Seventeen," Kelly answers, "but only ten alive right now." Salerno looks tired from a day of laying bricks and now taking night courses at the university to get a degree this late in life; Kelly collects a big disability for mental reasons, and so works when he wants to work, usually selling condo shares for beachfronts in the Carolinas. "It's hard to believe anything you say, Kelly," Salerno starts off, "fucking hard to believe anything you say, man." Salerno speaks in a whisper, what Kelly calls his friend's guido voice, so that no one at the table but

79

Kelly hears him. "True," Kelly says, "I exaggerate a little, that's true, but everything I'm saying happened, Sally." "Don't you fucking call me Sally, you potato-picking lush." It is as though Kelly does not hear his friend Salerno speaking; as though Kelly were lost in a long tunnel, or a fun house, or maybe drifting underwater like a kingfish. Then Kelly says: "Mo Phuc, Plei Boi, Firebase Screamin' Jesus." "Bleeding," Salerno corrects him, smiling evilly now. "Bleedin'," Kelly nods. "Why would I make this up, Sal?" "I don't know," Salerno says. "I just don't know, man."

YOUTH IN ASIA

On the Lower East Side, they called me Machine Gun, I worked in the library for awhile, bookstores, saloon kitchens, and even selling Xmas trees, had a beard real long, long hair, wore sneakers or Wellingtons in winter, work shirt, dungarees, p-coat, rolled my own, ate brown rice with tamari, knew a few well-off friends who bought the beer nightly, smoked aromatic Nepalese, attended poetry readings on Monday and Wednesday evenings, got into a few fistfights every once in a while, marched regularly against the goddamn war, where my cousins and childhood friends were buying the farm in great numbers when they were not terminating the indigenous personnel with extreme prejudice, it was not until, an adult, I went to Asia, married, with child, no one any longer called me Machine Gun, but rather Mr. Stephens, I had to laugh...

SPARROWS

Dull tan, homeless, bleached brown, some even brindled, there is perpetual vagrancy to them, as though their only purpose were to cadge quarters from passersby, or ask for a cup of coffee. Little grubbers shuffling the winter lawns, fly, scatter! In paintings or poetry they are quite beautiful, but in life nothing more than another form in motion. In that state, they are not unlike the destitute who photograph so well around Christmas...

THE SKATING POND

Legend had it that the pond was bottomless, and fed from an underground spring, but a friend once walked out to its center in August and it was just above his mouth at the midpoint as he stood on his toes, one of the biggest, dumbest kids in the fifth grade. When the pavement got wet from the night's rain, it iced over by morning, and after school I walked the half-mile to the skating pond, threw a potato into the fire and laced up my skates, letting the smell of wood and old leaves perfume the winter air, and later the mickey. At one end the older boys played hockey, and I contented myself with racing back and forth, skating backward in a zigzag pattern, then racing forward again, until my blade caught the rut in the ice, my ankle bent, I tripped over, coming down all wrong on my ankle—*snap*—I heard it fracture. A man wearing speed skates carried me off the ice, and drove me home in his yellow Cadillac coupe de ville, and I forgot all about the potato burning in the wood and leaf fire near the bare elm at the edge of the skating pond, and the hockey players.

WHISKEY

I bought a bottle of Bushmills at the local liquor store for the New Year's celebration, a half-gallon jug, and it disappeared in February, so I bought another. The next month my birthday came and went, and so I bought another still, things to do, like her concert, the conference, getting the taxes in order, after the last six-pack I ordered another bottle for the apartment, and I drank a glass of Irish to the general goodness of mankind, I drank to the Irish, Italians, Jews, Blacks, Hispanics, and I drank a glass to me and you. Here's to April, I said, or your sister who graduates in May, to June brides, our nation's independence, to the Assumption, the Ascension, to Mary's birth, and the feast of St. Francis. To Thanksgiving, to Christmas Eve, and yet another New Year's day. Here's to the old gang, the new gang, the old days, to the days ahead. And old loves, to whatsher-name, to your dog...

RELATIVITY

You let in light from the window, and it speeds into the room, at an impossible tilt and velocity. Not so much the threshold of speed, how it happens, but it happens, because it is that time of year before the winter solstice, when everything is a shadow, long and drifting in the amber light of first winter cold, it makes you consider at just what a grand speed light travels and even unravels before our eyes. By the calendar, winter is only another day away, only the light of this day proves there are not inter-actions in nature that are instant. Atoms freeze. Hear them tin-gle like chimes. Their roots coagulate and congeal. The sum of this is the universe we live in, and as we race toward light, watch us grow young and how things bend in toward us...

STILL LIFE WITH ANJOU PEAR

1. *The Chinese Bowl*

Pick up the pear, hold it in your hand, look at it, think of its sections, its parts, bite into it. Notice the aroma. Do not eat the seeds. Each half, eat, savoring the flavor. Now you know something about pears.

Amid pine and sycamore, on a shaded green lawn, lay out the blanket, the one you bought in Mexico, and on it place the peasant bread, wine glasses, plates of cheese (something with funk and humanity), a Chinese bowl with deviled eggs, and the half bottle of Cabernet Sauvignon from California. Doesn't matter what year. In the center of this, place a pear.

In one week the television announced that the tomato was not a vegetable, rather a fruit, and the pear turned into a woman. The painter writes: "I am an apple and I am a man. I am a man who thinks himself an apple. This happened when she announced herself to be a pear. She is a pear and she is a woman. When Eve tempted Adam with her naked apple. When you tempt me with your pear."

2. *Workshop Sketches of a Pear*

The sun hangs low, like a blazing orange, making long shadows on the green lawn, while the gray sky whirls, and through some trick of the eye, the pear casts the longest shadow, haunting me with its shades of brown and tan.

Eat, drink, draw. Take the pulp in hand. Study it. Linger on its pith. Smell the beads of juice. Break it open. Contemplate it. Eat and be captivated. Now draw it, the other one in the bowl. When he holds the pear in his hand, it is a pear, it does not move or speak. He contemplates it. But, again, on the blanket, it turns into a woman, perplexing him. He always liked apples, and he has not smelled a pear like this before, nor tasted one quite like it. It is not an apple. It is a pear. It is not a chair. It has hair, arms, legs, navel, fingers, toes, it has an angular nose, it sweats, it breathes.

The painter writes: "This spring I vow not to talk of love but only taste bitter herbs, to proclaim it is like winter, wet and cold, except that red maple is full of buds and the black oak runs with sap, and beyond the old outbuildings greeny clots of apple leaves break, pink geraniums bulge through the brown compost along the trail side near the white lichens, all harbingers of season, I guess, and the changes the world goes through, of the bulb-swell underground, its explosion, as root pokes deeper into ground-rot of woods, leached soil, and it is finally spring again, only where is my linkage to it—a painter, a man, a person—with these forms of life more alive than syntax and dendrons, more real than verbiage, synapse and pause, and so you take my hand, and we run through it, like another take from a scene in a movie, off with your hat and scarf, off with these shoes and socks, off with it, I say, and into this bed of rotting leaves..."

3. *Study for the Nude with the Bowl of Pears*

Stretch marks, wrinkles and puckers traverse her abdomen, her dugs pulled and torn, mouthed out of shape by lovers and children, and a neat incision cuts laterally over her genitals, and yet what she possesses is so human as to create tears as you attempt to sketch her. The parts of the buttock, of flank and calf, the greeny knot of vein and cellulite. What really intrigues you are the angles she possesses and holds or does not possess but has the potential to reveal by her imagination, the angle of light, and the pose she takes and holds. Her mouth with the sensuous pucker, and those eyes like black stars, her vaguely noble face bones and nose, her flowing black hair—make you notice her. If it were not for this sketch pad, the activity of plane and circle and arc, counterpoise and shading, she would be naked instead of a nude study. Shading and tone make age drop from her flanks, her uplifted face beckons, her nipples are hard and her breasts swell, making your pulse race and your skin feel like a million pinpricks. This is the one, you say, this is the one I must not only sketch but paint. So that it is only later, her robe on and fastened and she smoking a cigarette and chatting with the others around her, you remember to sketch in the bowl of pears beside her form.

4. *His Dream of a Red Studio*

Consider this paint's color which I have blended on the palette, maple leaves in a falling garden, part umber, part brown, the tan and flamboyan (a color of my own invention). I wear a tie I borrowed from a fellow painter, and I remember this green lawn, the sycamores, that blanket from the Yucatan, the bowl, glasses, bread, wine, pears. The trick is to paint it in a way to conjure other things and persons not on the canvas. The secret is to make "their" eyes feel the way you feel when she is around you.

I recall that the great painter in his red studio said: "Mes courbes ne sont pas folles." I recall how his mistress sat in a chair, her hat and hair a rainbow of colors. I recall the filigrees and hushed fillips, the red twists and the dazzling curlicues. I recall the Persian rugs, Moroccan tapestry, the odalisque with red musk. Do you recall that he did not paint "things," but the "difference" between things. Persimmon and lemon, saxifrages and orange. Blue flowers and the nu bleu. An ear of rye, blue tablecloth, clematis—doves...

5. *Peach Variation*

If I unbutton this button, the peach is a woman, and she has peach breasts. If I say nothing, she is a woman, perhaps peach, perhaps not. If I remind myself that peaches and cream are delicious, I can almost taste how good it is, smell it, touch it, roll around—like a turnover, say—and wear peaches like an overcoat. If I dare say this, the peach might be revealed. If there were time, for instance, an hour of this, two hours of that, to strip the peach, ah! This bewitches me.

6. *Blossoms*

If you plant a seed, often it will blossom, and those not coming to form go to seed in the fallow ground, but there are times when you plant and don't expect anything, when suddenly everything blossoms, even in December, in the hard ground, and it breaks through its bulb, bursting to the surface like a smile...

7. *Peach Blossoms*

You remove your blouse, step out of your skirt, and come naked to me. Peach blossoms fall.

8. *Peaches Are Not Pears*

Did I say peaches, I meant pears, though my mouth did not touch them, your smells made me believe their taste. They were a handful of pears. Did I say pears? I meant something else. What? You know. You guess. Round and shapely, small and soft. I was like an apple. Did I say pears? I meant, I meant to say, that is I said, only I forget, I forgot, I have forgotten, I meant to say…

9. *The Pear*

If he held the pear, and it became a woman, would she object to being held like that? He thinks of the pear again. And again. And again, he studies the objects on the blanket. By now the sky has changed and the light is different. The wine bottle. The cheese. The glasses. The bread. The eggs. The pear. The bowl. He prepares to finish the final sketch of the still life with pear. He holds the pencil and paper in his hands. He studies what is in front of him. Again, the pear turns into a woman. Draw, she says. He draws.